The Little Black Dog

◆ *BUCCANEER* ◆

by J. B. SPOONER

Illustrations by

TERRE LAMB SEELEY

ARCADE PUBLISHING · NEW YORK

Library of Congress Cataloging-in-Publication Data

Spooner, J. B.
The little Black Dog buccaneer / by J. B. Spooner ;
illustrations by Terre Lamb Seeley. — 1st ed.
p.   cm.
Summary: The famous Black Dog of Martha's Vineyard goes treasure hunting
and becomes a heroine on Captain Bob Douglas's schooner, the *Shenandoah*.
ISBN 978-1-61145-000-2
1. Black Dog (Dog)—Juvenile literature.   2. Douglas, Robert—
Juvenile literature.   3. Dogs—Massachussetts—Martha's Vineyard—
Biography—Juvenile literature.   [1. Black Dog (Dog)
2. Douglas, Robert.   3. Dogs.   4. Martha's Vineyard (Mass.)]
I. Seeley, Terre Lamb, ill.   II. Title.
SF426.5.S6635   1998
636.7'0886—dc21   98-21595

Arcade Publishing is an imprint of Skyhorse Publishing.

10 9 8 7 6 5 4 3

Printed in China through Asia Pacific Offset

To those who keep the legends of the sea alive

and pass them on to our children

It was winter in Vineyard Haven on the island of Martha's Vineyard. The tourist season was over, and Captain Douglas's schooner, the *Shenandoah*, was laid up till spring.

The little black dog, the orphaned pup that Captain Douglas had taken in, was happily settled in their home overlooking the harbor.

Captain Douglas and the little black dog belonged together.
Wherever the captain went, he always wore his favorite blue hat
and always had the little black dog at his side.

Winter days slipped easily by, working in the boat shop
by the warmth of the wood stove.

Evenings were spent by the fire with friends. Ever since the captain was a boy, he loved stories about pirate ships and sunken treasure. And for him, a good sea story was still the best way to pass a cold winter's night.

He liked nothing better than lying around the fire, swapping sea stories with his crew while the little black dog lay close by.

"Where'd she get her name?" asked Scotty, the first mate on the *Shenandoah*.

"I named her after the pirate Black Dog, in *Treasure Island*," the captain explained.

Throughout the winter, as the little black dog grew, so did her spirit of adventure. She learned how to jump up on the kitchen door and raise the latch with her two front paws. This meant she could come and go as she pleased. And she did.

She made friends easily and soon had a regular route about town.

Early in the morning she would head down to the Steamboat Dock to see her friend Bernie.

Then on to C. B. Stark's storefront for a visit with Grace Duffy.

After a quick tour through the A&P, she strolled up Main Street,

getting a smile from Ann at the bookstore . . .

and a pat from Shirley at the hardware store.

Bruce and Brandy at the flea market often introduced her to their customers.

And David, the checkout clerk at Cronig's Market, always <u>had</u> a treat waiting for her.

On her way home, she cut through Sally Knight's yard on the chance that another soup bone was being tossed out.

But the little black dog was more than just a friendly sailor in a friendly port. Most of all, she loved to search for buried treasure . . .

and she looked for it all over town.

She found
jewels at
the fishmarket . . .

silver at the school
playground . . .

treasure at the town hall . . .

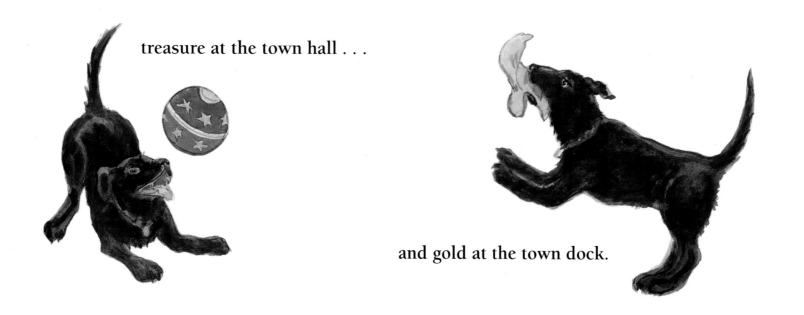

and gold at the town dock.

And when she discovered
buried treasure . . . she also
found the dog officer.

At first John Rogers tried to change her pirating ways, but he soon gave up.
Searching for buried treasure came as naturally to her as scratching an itch.

Whenever he saw her, he would stop his car and open the door.
She would drop whatever she was doing and hop in to be escorted home.

As spring approached and the days grew longer, the captain and his crew had many chores to do to get ready for the coming summer: splicing lines, varnishing blocks, painting the yawl boat.

Soon it was time to take the *Shenandoah* to Kelley's Shipyard in Fairhaven to be fitted out for the season. She was towed there by the tugboat *Jaguar*.

Black Dog liked to ride in the pilothouse with Charlie, the skipper of the tug. She sat in the skipper's chair and stuck her head out the window. "Sailing her ears," the crew would call it.

At Kelley's Shipyard, Charlie moved the *Shenandoah* alongside the wharf, where she was ready to be hauled out of the water.

Once the schooner was up on the railway, it took at least a week to scrape and paint her bottom. The captain examined her hull plank by plank.

The little black dog couldn't get up and down the ladder by herself. She barked to be carried up and she barked to be carried down.

When the *Shenandoah* was back in the water, the little black dog was able to come and go on her own. While the captain and crew painted the topsides and varnished all the brightwork, she settled into a routine.

Town Hall

Millicent Library

MARINE AN

She had discovered there was one thing
every sea port had in common—they all
had buried treasure. . .

and she was just the
clever pirate to find it.

Unitarian Church

Fairhaven
High School

Each time she returned, she brought some treasure back with her, and the crew began logging her bounty.

First she brought a leaf, then an old wooden chisel . . . then some sandpaper . . . sunglasses . . . and an old watch cap. One day she came back carrying a bright red bandanna, wagging her tail in delight.

"She's a pirate in the making, mark my words," said the bos'n with a grin. "And the *Shenandoah* is going to be known as a pirate ship."

LOG BOOK

April 19, Black Dog brought
in her first booty-
a pair of sunglasses!

April 20, Today, a ragged
blue watch cap. what to-
morrow?

LOG BOOK

On the last night at the boatyard, as Captain Douglas and his crew were getting ready to go to the Driftwood for a bowl of chowder, a policeman stood on the dock.

"You Captain Douglas?"

"Yes, sir. What can I do for you?"

"Your dog?" the dog officer asked, pointing to his car. In the backseat sat the little black dog.

"Caught her with a whole chicken, package and all," said the policeman with a chuckle. "When I stopped my car, she came right over and jumped in. I read her tag and called John Rogers in Vineyard Haven. Seems they're old friends.

"Rogers said, 'No need to look up her number. If you have a little black dog from Vineyard Haven looting in your town . . .

then you have a big white topsail schooner somewhere in your harbor.'"

"It's our little black buccaneer," laughed the crew.

"Maybe I shouldn't have named her after the pirate in *Treasure Island*," said Captain Douglas. He turned to the officer.

"I'd be happy to pay for the chicken," he said.

"No need. Just keep your pirate there under control," replied the officer.

"It's a good thing we're leaving or you'd end up in the brig," the captain scolded.

Next morning, Charlie and the tug *Jaguar* helped the *Shenandoah* get under-way early. They towed her to Vineyard Sound, where she had a fair breeze and a fair tide.

"Okay, let 'er go!" hollered Charlie as the crew dropped the hawser and waved good-bye.

The captain was happy to be heading home. His crew was eager to be sailing again, the hardest work of the season was behind them, and the "little black buccaneer" had escaped the pound.

The captain left Scotty at the wheel and went forward to inspect his vessel. A gust of wind whipped off his hat and lofted it into the air. His favorite hat!

Suddenly the sails were backing and the vessel was coming about.

"What's happening?" yelled the captain. He hadn't given any orders to tack. Scotty was pointing to something off the stern. The captain squinted in that direction.

It was the little black dog. Her head was bobbing
in the waves, barely a speck in the water.
"Dog overboard!" Scotty yelled.

The crew lowered the yawl boat. The captain jumped aboard and headed off the starboard quarter.

The little black dog was swimming furiously toward the schooner, looking very tired and very scared. As soon as the captain reached her, he scooped her out of the water. She had something in her mouth.

It was his favorite hat, clenched firmly in her teeth.
He held her in his arms and headed back to the schooner.

The crew cheered as the captain handed her over the side.
They passed her from arm to arm, each giving her an affectionate pat.
She was cold and shivering, but wagging her tail.
"Well," said the captain as he climbed back aboard and
proudly held up her latest bounty, "maybe her treasure hunting
comes in handy after all!"

Glossary of Sailing Terms

Back: to fill sails with wind on the opposite side from which they were originally set

Block: a casing through which lines are run

Bos'n: boatswain, or the officer next in command after the mate

Bounty: a reward

Bowsprit: the large spar extending forward from the bow of a ship

Brig: the place on a ship where prisoners are kept

Brightwork: woodwork that is varnished instead of painted

Buccaneer: a pirate

Chisel: a tool with a cutting edge for shaping wood

Come about: to tack

Fair breeze: a wind blowing favorably in direction and speed for a ship's course

Fair tide: an ocean current going in the same direction as a vessel

Fit out: to make ready

Hawser: a large rope used in towing or mooring

Hull: the frame or body of a ship

Lay up: to put away

Line: a length of rope used for any purpose

Log: to record in a ship's log

Mate: the officer who ranks second in command below the captain

Pilothouse: an enclosed place on the deck of a vessel for the steering gear and the helmsman

Pirate: one who robs at sea or on the shores of the sea

Plank: a long, flat piece of timber used for a vessel's hull

Quarter: the after (back) part of a ship's side

Railway: a line of rails forming a road that runs into the water

Schooner: a vessel with two or more masts and a fore-and-aft rig

Splice: to join together two parts of a rope by interweaving the strands

Starboard: the right side of a vessel facing forward

Stern: the hinder or rear part of a ship

Tack: to change the course of the ship by bringing her bow up into the wind and falling off on the opposite side

Topsail: a square sail on the top of a square-rigged vessel

Topsides: the upper part of a boat, above the water line

Treasure Island: a novel by Robert Louis Stevenson (1850–1894)

Tugboat: a strong, heavily powered vessel for towing other vessels

Watch cap: a knitted wool hat

Yawl boat: a ship's small boat